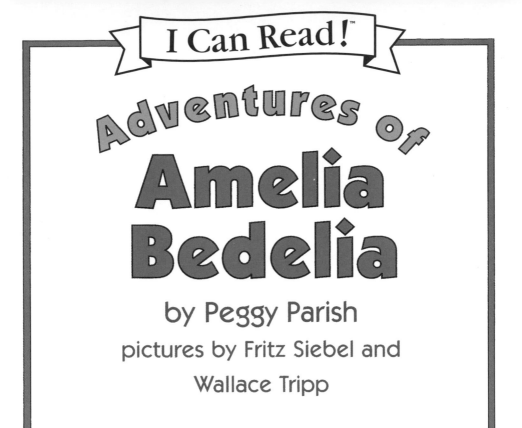

I Can Read!™

Adventures of Amelia Bedelia

by Peggy Parish

pictures by Fritz Siebel and
Wallace Tripp

Amelia Bedelia

Come Back, Amelia Bedelia

Play Ball, Amelia Bedelia

BARNES & NOBLE BOOKS

NEW YORK

For Debbie, John Grier,

Walter, and Michael Dinkins

Amelia Bedelia

"Oh, Amelia Bedelia,

your first day of work,

and I can't be here.

But I made a list for you.

You do just what the list says,"

said Mrs. Rogers.

Mrs. Rogers got into the car

with Mr. Rogers.

They drove away.

"My, what nice folks.

I'm going to like working here,"

said Amelia Bedelia.

Amelia Bedelia went inside.

"Such a grand house.

These must be rich folks.

But I must get to work.

Here I stand just looking.

And me with a whole list

of things to do."

Amelia Bedelia stood there

a minute longer.

"I think I'll make

a surprise for them.

I'll make lemon-meringue pie.

I do make good pies."

So Amelia Bedelia went
into the kitchen.
She put a little of this
and a pinch of that
into a bowl.
She mixed and she rolled.

Soon her pie was ready

to go into the oven.

"There," said Amelia Bedelia.

"That's done.

"Now let's see what this list says."

Amelia Bedelia read,

Change the towels in the green bathroom.

Amelia Bedelia found

the green bathroom.

"Those towels are very nice.

Why change them?" she thought.

17

Then Amelia Bedelia remembered

what Mrs. Rogers had said.

She must do just what

the list told her.

"Well, all right,"

said Amelia Bedelia.

Amelia Bedelia got some scissors.

She snipped a little here

and a little there.

And she changed those towels.

"There," said Amelia Bedelia.

She looked at her list again.

Dust the furniture.

"Did you ever hear tell

of such a silly thing.

At my house we undust the furniture.

But to each his own way."

20

Amelia Bedelia took

one last look at the bathroom.

She saw a big box with the words

Dusting Powder on it.

"Well, look at that.

A special powder to dust with!"

exclaimed Amelia Bedelia.

So Amelia Bedelia

dusted the furniture.

"That should be dusty enough.

My, how nice it smells."

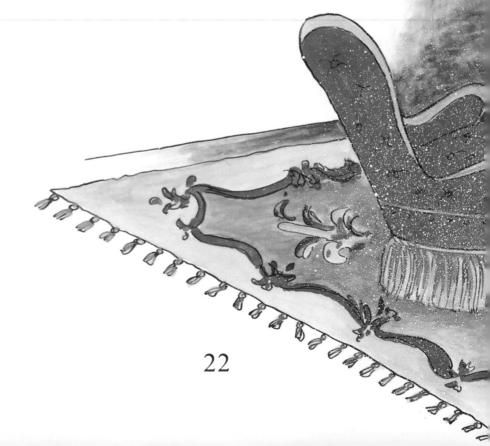

Draw the drapes when the sun comes in.

read Amelia Bedelia.

She looked up.

The sun was coming in.

Amelia Bedelia looked

at the list again.

"Draw the drapes?

That's what it says.

I'm not much

of a hand at drawing,

but I'll try."

So Amelia Bedelia sat right down
and she drew those drapes.

Amelia Bedelia

marked off

about the drapes.

"Now what?"

Put the lights out when you finish in the living room.

28

Amelia Bedelia
thought about this a minute.
She switched off the lights.
Then she carefully
unscrewed each bulb.

And Amelia Bedelia
put the lights out.
"So those things need
to be aired out, too.
Just like pillows and babies.
Oh, I do have a lot to learn."

"My pie!" exclaimed Amelia Bedelia.
She hurried to the kitchen.

"Just right," she said.

She took the pie out of the oven

and put it on the table to cool.

Then she looked at the list.

Measure two cups of rice.

"That's next," said Amelia Bedelia.

Amelia Bedelia found two cups.

She filled them with rice.

34

And Amelia Bedelia

measured that rice.

Amelia Bedelia laughed.

"These folks

do want me to do funny things."

Then she poured the rice

back into the container.

The meat market will deliver a steak and a chicken.

Please trim the fat before you put the steak in the icebox.

And please dress the chicken.

When the meat arrived,

Amelia Bedelia opened the bag.

She looked at the steak

for a long time.

"Yes," she said.

"That will do nicely."

Amelia Bedelia got some lace

and bits of ribbon.

And Amelia Bedelia

trimmed that fat

before she put

the steak in the icebox.

"Now I must dress the chicken.

I wonder if she wants

a he chicken or a she chicken?"

said Amelia Bedelia.

Amelia Bedelia went right to work.

Soon the chicken was finished.

Amelia Bedelia heard the door open.

"The folks are back," she said.

She rushed out to meet them.

"Amelia Bedelia,

why are all the light bulbs outside?"

asked Mr. Rogers.

"The list just said

to put the lights out,"

said Amelia Bedelia.

"It didn't say to bring them back in.

Oh, I do hope

they didn't get aired too long."

47

"Amelia Bedelia,

the sun will fade the furniture.

I asked you to draw the drapes,"

said Mrs. Rogers.

"I did! I did! See,"

said Amelia Bedelia.

She held up her picture.

Then Mrs. Rogers saw the furniture.

"The furniture!" she cried.

"Did I dust it well enough?"

asked Amelia Bedelia.

"That's such nice dusting powder."

Mr. Rogers went to wash his hands.

"I say," he called.

"These are very unusual towels."

Mrs. Rogers dashed into the bathroom.

"Oh, my best towels," she said.

"Didn't I change them enough?"

asked Amelia Bedelia.

53

Mrs. Rogers went to the kitchen.

"I'll cook the dinner.

Where is the rice

I asked you to measure?"

"I put it back in the container.

But I remember—

it measured four and a half inches,"

said Amelia Bedelia.

55

"Was the meat delivered?"

asked Mrs. Rogers.

"Yes," said Amelia Bedelia.

"I trimmed the fat just like you said.

It does look nice."

Mrs. Rogers rushed to the icebox.

She opened it.

"Lace! Ribbons!

Oh, dear!" said Mrs. Rogers.

"The chicken—you dressed

the chicken?"

asked Mrs. Rogers.

"Yes, and I found the nicest box

to put him in,"

said Amelia Bedelia.

"Box!" exclaimed Mrs. Rogers.

Mrs. Rogers hurried over to the box.

She lifted the lid.

There lay the chicken.

And he was just as dressed

as he could be.

59

Mrs. Rogers was angry.

She was very angry.

She opened her mouth.

Mrs. Rogers meant

to tell Amelia Bedelia

she was fired.

But before she could

get the words out,

Mr. Rogers put something

in her mouth.

It was so good

Mrs. Rogers forgot about being angry.

"Lemon-meringue pie!"

she exclaimed.

"I made it to surprise you,"

said Amelia Bedelia happily.

So right then and there

Mr. and Mrs. Rogers decided

that Amelia Bedelia must stay.

And so she did.

Mrs. Rogers learned to say

undust the furniture,

unlight the lights,

close the drapes,

and things like that.

Mr. Rogers didn't care

if Amelia Bedelia

trimmed all

of his steaks with lace.

All he cared about

was having her there

to make lemon-meringue pie.

Come Back, Amelia Bedelia

For my favorite people
on 10 West
Judy Freedman
Jeanne Chernay
Rosemary Friedman
With much love-

"Oh, my cream puffs!"

said Amelia Bedelia.

She went to the stove.

"Just right," she said.

Amelia Bedelia took her cream puffs

out of the stove.

5

"There now," she said.

"I'll just let them cool.

Then I will fill them

with chocolate cream."

Mrs. Rogers came into the kitchen.

"Good morning, Amelia Bedelia,"

she said.

6

"Good morning," said Amelia Bedelia.

"I will have some cereal

with my coffee this morning,"

said Mrs. Rogers.

"All right," said Amelia Bedelia.

Mrs. Rogers went into the dining room.

Amelia Bedelia got the cereal.

She put some in a cup.

And she fixed Mrs. Rogers

some cereal with her coffee.

8

She took it into the dining room.

"Amelia Bedelia!" said Mrs. Rogers.

"What is that mess?"

"It's your cereal with coffee,"

said Amelia Bedelia.

"Oh, you are impossible!"

said Mrs. Rogers. "You're fired!"

"You mean you don't want me

anymore?" asked Amelia Bedelia.

"That is just what I mean,"

said Mrs. Rogers. "Now go!"

Amelia Bedelia

got her bag.

And she went away.

Amelia Bedelia walked toward town.

"Now what will I do?" she said.

She passed by the beauty shop.

A sign said **LADY WANTED**.

12

"Now let's see what that's about,"

said Amelia Bedelia.

She went into the beauty shop.

13

"Can I help you?" asked a lady.

"No, I came to help you,"

said Amelia Bedelia.

"Can you fix hair?" asked the lady.

14

"Oh yes," said Amelia Bedelia.

"I can do that."

"Then you can start now,"

said the lady. "Mrs. Hewes is waiting

to have her hair pinned up."

15

"All right," said Amelia Bedelia.

She looked all around.

"But I don't see any pins,"

she thought. "It's a good thing

I carry some with me."

Amelia Bedelia opened her purse.

She took out some pins.

17

And Amelia Bedelia began to pin up

Mrs. Hewes' hair.

"What are you doing!"

said Mrs. Hewes.

"Pinning up your hair,"

said Amelia Bedelia.

"Did I stick you?"

"Help!" called Mrs. Hewes.

The beauty shop lady came.

"Oh, no!" she said.

"What have you done?

Go away right this minute."

"All right," said Amelia Bedelia.

20

So Amelia Bedelia went on her way.

"Now why did she get so mad?"

said Amelia Bedelia.

"I just did what she told me to do."

Amelia Bedelia looked

in all the stores.

She came to a dress shop.

It had a **HELP WANTED** sign

in the window.

Amelia Bedelia went into the store.

"What kind of help is wanted?"

she asked.

"Sewing help," said the lady.

"Can you sew?"

"Yes," said Amelia Bedelia.

"I am very handy with a needle."

"Then come with me," said the lady.

She took Amelia Bedelia

into a back room.

"Please shorten these dresses.

They are already marked,"

said the lady.

"All right," said Amelia Bedelia.

The lady left her.

"I don't need to sew

to do this," said Amelia Bedelia.

She took the scissors.

And Amelia Bedelia shortened

those dresses.

Amelia Bedelia went back

to the front of the store.

"I'm finished," she said.

"What is next?"

"Finished!" said the lady.

"How could you be?"

The lady went into the back room.

She saw the dresses.

"Oh, no!" she said.

"You have ruined them."

"But I just shortened them,"

said Amelia Bedelia.

"Oh, go away," said the lady.

"I don't want you."

So Amelia Bedelia went.

"Some folks," she said,

"I just don't understand them."

Amelia Bedelia walked

another block or so.

She saw a sign in a window.

It said **FILE CLERK WANTED**.

"Now I wonder what a file clerk is,"

she said. "I'll just go in and find out."

34

A man met her.

"Are you a file clerk?" he asked.

"I will be one," said Amelia Bedelia,

"if you will tell me what to do."

"All right," said the man.

"First, take these letters.

They need stamps.

Then file these papers."

"I'll do that," said Amelia Bedelia.

The man went into his office.

Amelia Bedelia looked at the letters.

"Now should I stamp them all at once

or one at a time?" she thought.

"I better do them one at a time."

So Amelia Bedelia took each letter.

She put it on the floor.

And Amelia Bedelia stamped on it.

"There," she said.

"That should be enough stamps.

Now I better get these papers filed."

Amelia Bedelia looked at the papers.

Then she looked in her purse.

She found a fingernail file.

"It sure is small

to file all these papers.

But I will do the best I can."

And Amelia Bedelia began

to file the papers.

41

The man came back.

"Stop!" he said. "What are you doing!"

"Just filing your papers,"

said Amelia Bedelia.

"Do you have a bigger file?"

"Oh, no!" said the man.

"Do go away."

So Amelia Bedelia went.

"I declare!" she said.

"Everybody is mad today."

Amelia Bedelia

walked on down the street.

She came to a doctor's office.

There was a sign that said

HELP WANTED.

"Maybe that's the job for me,"

said Amelia Bedelia.

She went inside.

The doctor was there.

"I will be your help,"

said Amelia Bedelia.

"Good," said the doctor.

"Bring in the patients one at a time.

Come when I buzz for you."

46

"All right," said Amelia Bedelia.

"I can do that."

The doctor went into his office.

A woman and a girl came in.

"Who is the patient?"

asked Amelia Bedelia.

"Jane," said the woman.

47

"Then I'll take her in,"

said Amelia Bedelia.

She picked Jane up.

"Put me down! I can walk!"

screamed Jane.

"Nope," said Amelia Bedelia,

"the doctor said to bring you in."

And Amelia Bedelia carried Jane

into the doctor's office.

49

"Put Jane down!" said the doctor.

"Bring her mother in."

"Bring her mother in?"

said Amelia Bedelia.

"Can't she just walk?"

"Never mind," said the doctor.

"Mrs. Jackson, please come in."

Amelia Bedelia went back to her desk.

51

A little later the buzzer rang.

"I need your help," said the doctor.

"Dickie has a bad cut.

He needs a few stitches."

"I can take care of that,"

said Amelia Bedelia.

She opened her purse.

"Here is a needle. Now,

what color thread does Dickie like?"

"No! No!" said the doctor.

"I wanted you to put my gloves on.

Can you do that?"

"Oh my, yes!" said Amelia Bedelia.

"I will be glad to."

So Amelia Bedelia

put the doctor's gloves on.

"There now," she said.

"They're a little big,

but they're on. What next?"

The doctor looked at Amelia Bedelia.

His face turned red.

"Go home!" he said.

"Home!" said Amelia Bedelia.

"My goodness!" she said.

"I forgot about my cream puffs.

I must go back and fill them."

Amelia Bedelia went back

to the Rogers house.

"I'll just make the chocolate cream,"

said Amelia Bedelia.

She put a little of this

and a bit of that into a pot.

She mixed and she stirred.

And soon her chocolate cream

was cooked.

Mrs. Rogers came into the kitchen.

"That smells good," she said.

"Well," said Amelia Bedelia,

"I'll just fill the cream puffs.

Then I will be on my way."

"Oh, no!" said Mrs. Rogers.

"I'm sorry I got mad.

Please come back, Amelia Bedelia.

We miss you."

"All right," said Amelia Bedelia.

"I will be glad to."

61

Mr. Rogers came into the kitchen.

"I'm hungry," he said.

"Amelia Bedelia,

please heat me a can of soup."

"All right," said Amelia Bedelia.

She took a can of soup.

She put it in a pot.

And Amelia Bedelia

heated that can of soup.

64

Play Ball, Amelia Bedelia

for Jamie Murphy,
one of my favorite young friends,
with love

Amelia Bedelia walked by

the baseball field.

The Grizzlies team was there.

5

"I never saw such gloomy faces,"

said Amelia Bedelia.

"Did something terrible happen?"

6

"We play the Tornados today,"
said Jimmy.

"And Donny has the measles."

"There is no one
to take his place," said Tom.

7

"What about me?" said Amelia Bedelia.

"You!" said the boys. "Great!"

"But I don't know much

about the game," said Amelia Bedelia.

"I will explain it to you," said Tom.

"The idea of the game

is to hit the ball

and run to each of the bases.

8

The other team tries to get the ball

and tag you out," he said.

"That is easy enough,"

said Amelia Bedelia.

9

"Maybe we should warm her up

at bat," said Bob.

"Good idea," said Tom.

"Amelia Bedelia, you hit the ball

when Bob throws it."

"All right," she said.

Bob pitched the ball,

but Amelia Bedelia missed it.

"No, no," said Tom.

"You must step in

to meet the ball."

Bob pitched the ball again.

And Amelia Bedelia stepped in

to meet it.

"Ouch!" she said. "This game hurts!"

13

The boys taught Amelia Bedelia

how to bat.

Later she said, "All right,

I'm warmed up. In fact, I am hot."

"Then be here at two o'clock,"

said Jimmy. "The game starts then."

Amelia Bedelia went home.

She went right up to the attic.

"I know there is a uniform here,"

said Amelia Bedelia.

And there was one.

She took a nip here and a tuck there.

Soon that uniform was just right.

"That's done," said Amelia Bedelia.

"Now what should I do

until it is time to go?"

Then she saw the cookie jar.

"It's empty!" she said.

"Well, I will soon fix that."

Amelia Bedelia put some of this

and a bit of that into a bowl.

Amelia Bedelia mixed and she rolled.

Soon her cookies were all baked.

"There now," she said.

"That's done."

Amelia Bedelia looked at the clock.

"My goodness!" she said.

"I better be on my way."

Amelia Bedelia got her things

and went to the ball park.

"Here she is!

Here's Amelia Bedelia!"

called the Grizzlies.

"Then let's play ball,"

said the Tornados.

19

"The Tornados are up first,"
said Tom.

"Amelia Bedelia, you stand here.

Catch the ball if it comes your way."

"All right," she said.

"Batter up!" called the pitcher.

The pitcher threw the ball.

The batter hit it.

He ran to first base.

"Get the ball, Amelia Bedelia,"
yelled Tom. "Tag Jack
before he gets to second base."

22

"I must have a tag in here

somewhere," said Amelia Bedelia.

She tagged Jack.

23

Another boy came up to bat.

He hit the ball.

The ball landed near Amelia Bedelia.

"Throw it to first base,"
yelled the boys. "Put Dick out."
So Amelia Bedelia threw the ball
to first base.

25

Then she ran and grabbed Dick.
"How far out do you want him?"
she called.

"Amelia Bedelia!" shouted the boys.

"Put him down."

So Amelia Bedelia put Dick down.

"You sure do change your minds fast,"

she said. "You told me

to put him out!"

Dick got back on first base.

And the game went on.

The next batter missed the ball.

The catcher threw the ball

to the pitcher.

The pitcher missed it.

But Amelia Bedelia caught it!

"Hurry, Amelia Bedelia!

Throw the ball!" shouted the boys.

"Dick is trying

to steal second base."

"Steal second base!"

said Amelia Bedelia.

"That's not nice."

31

Amelia Bedelia ran

and picked up second base.

"It's all right now, fellows,"

she called. "Second base is safe."

"For gosh sakes, Amelia Bedelia!"

said the boys. "Put that back."

Amelia Bedelia looked puzzled.

"But he was going to steal it,"

she said.

"It's all right to steal bases,"

said Tom.

"That is part of the game."

"Oh," said Amelia Bedelia.

Finally the Tornados were out.

They had made two runs.

It was the Grizzlies' turn at bat.

Tom was first.

He struck out.

34

Then Jimmy had his turn.

He hit that ball hard.

He made it to third base.

Next it was Bob's turn.

He hit the ball.

"Pop fly," called the pitcher.

"I've got it."

"Pop fly?" said Amelia Bedelia.

"I didn't hear anything pop!"

Then it was Amelia Bedelia's turn.

"Come on, Amelia Bedelia," said Bob.

"Make a base hit

so Jimmy can come in."

"Which base should I hit?" she asked.

Tom said, "Just hit the ball

and run to first base!"

"All right," said Amelia Bedelia.

And that is just what she did.

Jimmy scored for the Grizzlies.

The team cheered.

The next player struck out.

The Tornados were at bat again.

The score was

Tornados 2, Grizzlies 1.

The Grizzlies called a time-out.

"Amelia Bedelia is not very good

in the field," said Jimmy.

"She gets all mixed-up," said Tom.

"Maybe she could be catcher,"

said Bob.

The boys turned to Amelia Bedelia.

"You be the catcher," said Jimmy.

"What do I do?" she asked.

"Stand behind the batter

and catch the ball," said Jimmy.

"Then throw it back to the pitcher."

So Amelia Bedelia

stood behind the batter.

The pitcher threw the ball.

The batter was about to hit it.

But Amelia Bedelia pushed him

out of the way.

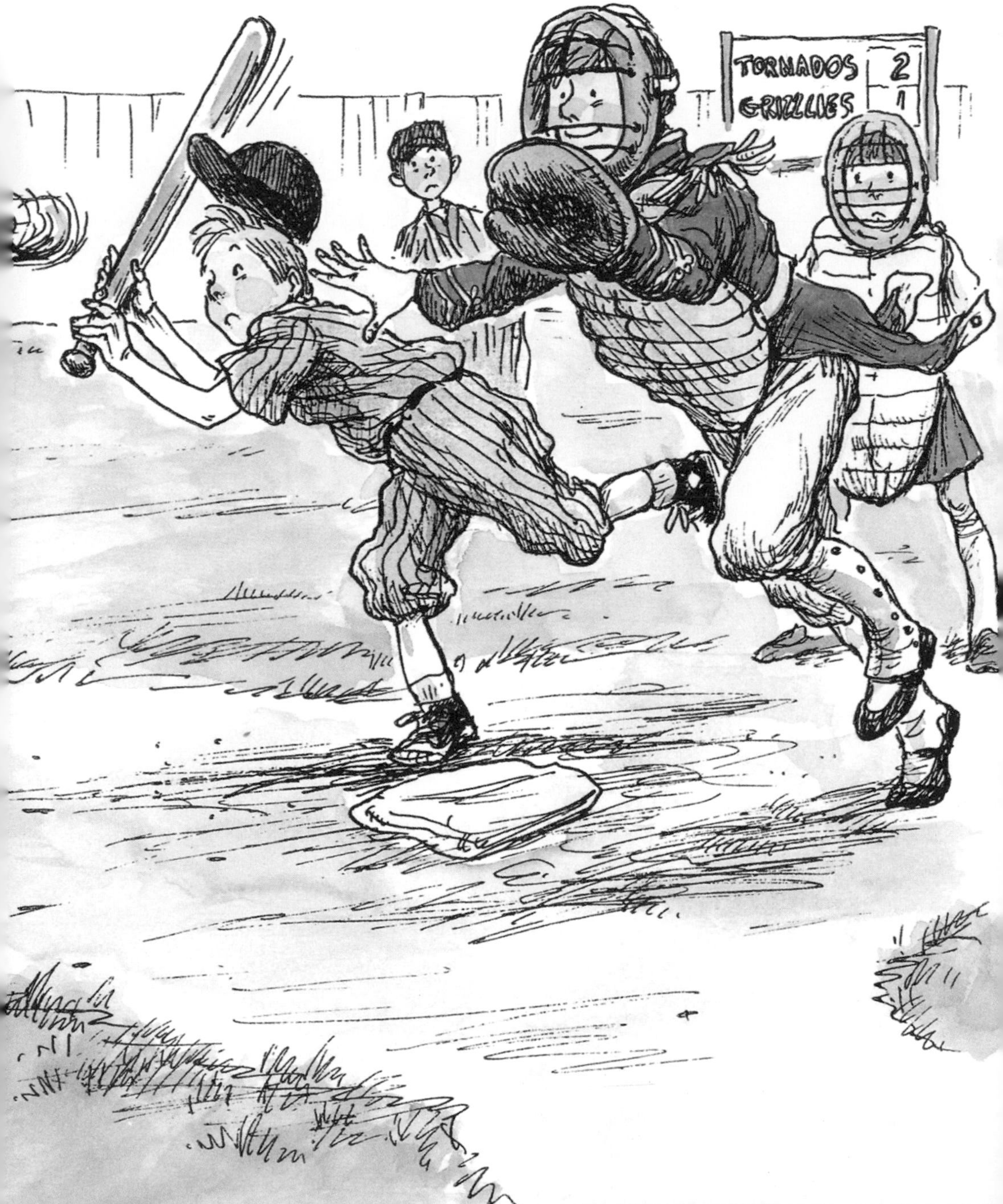
TORNADOS 2
GRIZZLIES 1

And Amelia Bedelia caught the ball.

"I got it, fellows!" she called.

The whole team groaned.

The Tornados were very angry.

"Put her someplace else,"
they shouted. "Put her way out."
So the Grizzlies put Amelia Bedelia
way out in the field.

The game was not going well

for the Grizzlies.

The score was

Tornados 8, Grizzlies 5.

The Grizzlies were at bat.

It was the last inning.

They had two outs.

The bases were loaded.

And Amelia Bedelia was at bat.

The Grizzlies were worried.

"Please, Amelia Bedelia," they said.

"Please hit that ball hard."

Amelia Bedelia

swung at the first ball.

She missed.

She swung at the second ball.

And again she missed.

"Please, Amelia Bedelia, please,"

shouted the Grizzlies.

Amelia Bedelia

swung at the next ball.

And oh, how she hit that ball!

"Run, Amelia Bedelia, run!"

yelled the boys.

"Run to first base."

And Amelia Bedelia ran.

"Tom says stealing

is all right," she said,

"so I'll just steal all the bases.

I will make sure the Grizzlies win."

Amelia Bedelia

scooped up first base,

and second base,

and third base.

"Home!" shouted the boys.

"Run home, Amelia Bedelia!"

Amelia Bedelia looked puzzled,

but she did not stop running.

And on her way she scooped up

home plate too.

The boys were too surprised

to say a thing.

Then Tom yelled, "We won!

We won the game!"

"Amelia Bedelia, come back!"

shouted the boys. "We won!"

But Amelia Bedelia was running

too fast to hear.

She did not stop

until she reached home.

"That is a silly game," she said.

"Having me run all the way home!"

Suddenly she heard a loud roar.

"Hurray! Hurray!

Hurray for Amelia Bedelia!"

There were the Grizzlies.

"We won! The score was

Grizzlies 9, Tornados 8,"

said Jimmy.

"You saved the game,

Amelia Bedelia."

"I'm glad I could help you boys out,"

said Amelia Bedelia.

"Maybe we should keep

Amelia Bedelia

on our team," said Bob.

"She could be our scorekeeper."

"I would be happy to keep

your score," said Amelia Bedelia.

58

"I have a nice box with a lock on it.

Your score would be safe with me."

The boys laughed.

"You will never learn baseball,"

said Tom. "Now can we please have

our bases and home plate back?"

"You sure can," said Amelia Bedelia.

59

Amelia Bedelia went inside.

She looked at home plate.

"Now what kind of a home

would use a plate like that?"

she said.

"But it isn't polite

to return an empty plate.

I will have to do something."

Amelia Bedelia looked at the cookies.

"That's it," she said.

Amelia Bedelia piled

home plate with cookies.

"Here you are fellows," she said.

The boys quickly emptied

home plate.

"Those are the best cookies

I ever ate," said Jimmy.

"Maybe Amelia Bedelia will never

learn baseball," said Tom,

"but she sure can cook."

"Hurray for Amelia Bedelia!

Hurray for her cookies!"

shouted the boys.

Then the boys went on their way.

And Amelia Bedelia

went in to bake.

That cookie jar

was empty again!